Adeline and the

The crimes and punishment of Mean

Moggie!

Be Kind

Be Honest

Share Love

Share Hope

 And you will shine like the brightest star!

Age 6yrs +

For Christopher

For giving me the courage!

It took many, many days. The artist poured all their love into the clay they were so carefully sculpting. The delicate hands, the tiny feet and the gossamer wings. Days and days past. Each day the artist continued to pour love into that tiny statue. One bright sunny morning the artist was pleased. The beautiful delicate fairy was finished. Her pure white glaze ready to be fired in the kiln. The artist had made her wings of bronze, golden and fine. They would fit after her days in the kiln.

The artist carefully places her wings of bronze and she was finished. Pure white and so very pretty sat upon a toadstool with bluebells around her feet. It was the artist's last piece, their eyes fading with age it would no longer be possible to make these wonderful sculptures any more.

That is when the magic came. The Fairy Folk or The Fae were soon drawn to this artist's work. They are curious tiny creatures, always bobbing and fluttering around, curious to the point of being quite nosey and quite often getting into all sorts of scrapes and trouble. The Fae were drawn to this tiny statue because they all felt the love that had been given to this tiny fairy and each night, they came to see the artist's work. How beautiful she was. When the Queen of the Fae heard the whispers of this beautiful statue she came to see with her own eyes. She fluttered around it and stared in wonder, truly this was a work of pure love. The clay, the glaze and bronze radiated love and so the Queen of the

Fae gave magic to this beautiful creation. The Queen of the Fae has the power to grant many wishes, though she rarely does so to humankind. She felt the Artist's love glowing all around this delicate, tiny creation and thought it was too much to waste such love. She thought she would grant this creation of love a blessing. The gift of life. For that is a true gift and blessing. Being the wise queen that she was she was careful in her gift. For magic has a price and should always be used with care! As more often than not wishes granted can turn into our worst nightmares!

So, she spoke the words and granted life to our tiny fairy.

'Those who look but do not see, those that hear but do not listen will only see you as you are, but one who looks and sees, who hears and listens and sees wonder in all of creation will see you and hear you! They will know your name!'

You see, a fairy will so very rarely tell their name to any human folk. Their name is granted by the Queen and is so very special to them. If they give their name to a human folk then it must be done with great care. Once you know a fairy's name you can call them to your bidding and a fairy well knows how human folk can be devious and mis-use their magics. Once a silly fairy granted her name to a greedy farmer. Each season he would call the fairy to use her magic to make his crops grow so much better than all the other farmers. The other farmers became suspicious and accused the farmer's beautiful, kind and loving wife of being a witch! And his poor wife was taken away, tried by the court and sentenced to death for being a witch. So that is why a fairy will hardly ever give a human folk their name, and quite rightly so. Magic has consequences as the greedy farmer found out and lost his most beloved wife!

So, it was to be that this tiny fairy was gifted with life and it would be a rare humankind that would befriend this tiny creature and share a bond that would last an eternity.

And so, the artist passed away with their last creation by their side and then our fairy was wrapped and packed and sent away.

But it was only the beginning of her journey!

'Oh Fred, look, look. Isn't that lovely?' June said as she peered into the 'Olde But Treasured Shoppe' in a quiet back street in Lincoln. Fred was busy eyeing the juicy pork pies in the butchers shop next door. 'Fred, come and look!'

Fred thought, 'OK, better look and then I can nip into the butchers and get one of those big fat pork pies to take home, mmm! Maybe a couple of those big T-Bone steaks would go down a treat too and he could do those nice new Jersey potatoes, salted and buttered. Yum. Better put some salad with it too, five a day and all!' But he said, 'OK sweetie, what you looking at?'

As you can gather Fred was rather fond of his food, and his large round belly paid homage to all those tasty dishes he cooked up in his kitchen, June on the other hand was a chocolate and cake kind of girl! But Fred was a good cook and so she had the best of both worlds. No cooking and a hubby that loved everything tasty! You see Fred and June had been together all their lives, married young and loved each other very much. But you see they were brought up after a great war that left people with very little, and their food was rationed by the government! But now they were getting on those days had passed and food and nice things were everywhere. So, there was Fred, round as a barrel and June well she was no waif either. They worked hard and now liked good food and nice things in their house. I am sure you can understand.

'Look, there tucked at the back. That tiny figurine of a fairy. It is so lovely!'

'Oh, yes I see it now. You really like it?' Fred said smiling at his wife. She loved to have nice things, though their new bungalow was getting a little crowded. 'Come on let's go inside, go on lass, get inside.' Fred chuckled, thinking it was rather lovely and more so thinking of that big fat pork pie waiting next door.

The 'Olde But Treasured Shoppe' was packed, floor to ceiling. Everything you could imagine lingered on shelves hoping for someone to come and take them out of the dusty, spider-webby, musty shop. I would like to point out that the owner, one Mr Jerimiah Jeffrey Johnson Jones, was just as dusty, spider-webby and musty as all the things in his shop. Though his clothes were of fine make, the moths had made a good meal of them at one time. Though his hair and beard were the colour of freshly laid snow and were washed and trimmed they seemed to have a determination to try and leap off his head and face. Like those cartoons when the cat sticks his tail in the electric socket, and well we all know the result of that! Skinny as a garden rake, with bright blue eyes that seemed to glow in the spider-webby, dusty and musty shop, Mr Jerimiah Jeffrey Johnson Jones was a man who could be relied upon, always kind and never ever would cheat or over charge his customers. I suppose that is why he would never have pots of gold, but his heart was the brightest gold anyone could wish for. He was as happy as anyone could be or would want to be, in his small town, in his small shop, crammed with everything that anyone could want!

'Welcome, welcome. Please come in and browse. We have many fine things to tempt you with.' Said Mr Jerimiah Jeffrey Johnson Jones, who was for all purposes, in this case we will call him 'a gentleman'.

He had fine manners and a very polite tongue. He held no sway with this modern, gobbley-gook that the youngsters spoke, all 'Hey bud' and text speak. But that was the way of the world, but that did not mean Mr Jerimiah Jeffrey Johnson Jones had to change, absolutely never, not even for a pot of gold would Mr Jerimiah Jeffrey Johnson Jones change.

He looked at his potential customers, both had lovely fresh smiling faces and both were, erm, large and very, very round. Mr Jerimiah Jeffrey Johnson

Jones had a fleeting thought of the rather round gentleman getting stuck between some shelves! But he would never, ever, ever be impolite to anyone! So, he stood guard, just in case that large round belly should knock over a shelf. Or become wedged between his tightly packed rows of shelves, just like a piece of ham between two slices of wholemeal bread!

'My wife, June, has seen a very lovely porcelain figurine in your window. At the back to the left….' Fred chirped to Mr Jerimiah Jeffrey Johnson Jones, and smiled at the rather untidy and very well-spoken young man before him. Ah you thought Mr Jerimiah Jeffrey Johnson Jones was an old creaky-bones? Well Mr Jerimiah Jeffrey Johnson Jones was just a mere chit at 40-years of age. Well, yes of course to you, 40 is ancient in fact more than ancient, Mega-Ancient, but to Fred who was, my dare I tell you, 60-years of age, Mr Jerimiah Jeffrey Johnson Jones was a mere youngster. So, Fred was a Mega-Mega-Ancient!

'Ah, yes. I know the piece.' In fact, Mr Jerimiah Jeffrey Johnson Jones knew every single item in his shop! So, he maybe a Mega-Ancient but he had a Mega-Memory-Mind. 'Just one moment and I will bring it over to the counter for your lovely wife.' And he set off, squeezing and squiggling and wriggling past bookcases and shelves filled with everything anyone could want. He came back covered in more dust, carefully squeezing and squiggling and wriggling past the bookcases and shelves filled with everything anyone could want. Fred and June watched and held their breath as many of the things that anyone could want wibbled and wobbled on those packed, rammed and crammed shelves.

'There, she is rather beautiful. She is signed and was made by quite a renowned local artist. In fact, it was the last piece ever made. His children had no care for anything but selling everything they could. I have a few of his sculptures. If it is not impolite, they were not very pleasant children at all. You would have thought one of them would want this, this perfect and most beautiful thing.'

'That is so sad,' Said June who was holding the delicate figure with a look of love in her eyes, 'it is so finely made, the bronze wings so delicate. I would never have thought that metal could be so fine and such a golden colour.'

'I think you have a sale, Sir.' Fred knew that there was no way, no how and no buts that his lovely wife was not leaving the 'Olde But Treasured Shoppe' without the figurine. Mind it was lovely so! 'How much would it be?'

'Well.' Mr Jerimiah Jeffrey Johnson Jones pondered. And thinking that he loved the tiny fairy, it was so beautiful and by look of the lady she would place it in her home, no doubt to be seen every day by her and all who visited their home. That pleased Mr Jerimiah Jeffrey Johnson Jones, he knew every item in his shop and cared only that they were purchased by customers who would cherish them. Mr Jerimiah Jeffrey Johnson Jones was a very sentimental and caring Mega-Ancient 40-year old gentleman. So, he pondered, this tiny fairy needed a warm and kind home and someone to dust her and look after her. Mr Jerimiah Jeffrey Johnson Jones was rather laxi-daisy at dusting!

'For you good lady, how does £10 seem. A special price of the day!' Mr Jerimiah Jeffrey Johnson Jones chirped and smiled.

'My goodness, are you sure? It seems so inexpensive....' June was absolutely astounded as she thought it must have been about £100!

'Err, June. If that is the price then, well I think, as we say in Sheffield, "Aye thinks that be a reet good baarrgain" and there will be no quibbling over that price.' Fred piped up, quickly fumbling for his wallet and taking out the £10. You see, Fred was a salesman and a very good salesman at that. He could sell snow to the Northern snow people and sand to the desert people. I think he could sell water to the Scots and we all know how much is rains in Scotland! So, Fred knew a very good bargain when he saw one, but his bonny lass, well she could save and squirrel away pennies for a rainy day, but was not much good at the age-old idea of a never quibble over a bargain when one is right in front of your eyes! Count the good fortune that has crossed your path.

'There you go sir, and thank you for the price. That tiny little fairy will be dearly cherished.' Said Fred, beaming at the absolutely great price and knowing his wallet was still fat with cash ready to rush to the very tasty butcher's shop next door!

'Well, then it is a very good day by all.' Said Mr Jerimiah Jeffrey Johnson Jones who was sad to see one of his items go, but cheered himself at the thought of it being in a nice home. 'Please, allow me to wrap her and find a nice safe box to take her home in.'

'While you wait for your package June, I will nip next door. The butcher's looks like a real nice one.' Said Fred, already on his way out the door, thinking of that big fat pork pie! Not forgetting the big juicy steaks as well. He also sneaked next door to 'Geraldine's Gorgeous, Scrumptious and Absolutely Delicious Cake shoppe' and picked out some of the most delicious strawberry tarts you could ever imagine. Dinner time was going to be truly fantastic!

And so, that is how fairy came to be with Fred and June in their new bungalow in the village of Ridgeway, not far from Sheffield. And a nice home it was too!

The years tick by, tick-tock, day by day, week by week, month by month and year by year. Fred and June have a good life, working hard, travelling all over the world and then retiring. Their three children grow up and go out to live their lives. New arrivals come along, grand-children and then great grand-children. It is one of these great grand-children that has the gift to see the magic that the Queen of the Fae granted the Fairy. And it is where our story really begins.

And all this time Fairy sits on the fire place mantle, watching over this family. Though no one sees her in her magical form, she is no less loved and cared for. Her home is always warm and snug, sunny and bright. She watches over them, watches over her home. Through the window she sees the Garden Fae, busy doing all things that nature intended them to do. Making sure the snails and slugs don't eat the blue biscuits. The Fairy knows the blue biscuits are bad, just one tiny nibble and a poor snail or slug will melt like wax. But June does not like to use the blue biscuits, so she picks up the snails and puts them across the road in the hedgerows. What she does not know, snails are clever. They simply turn around, cross the busy road and come back into her garden during the night. Why at night? Well when you are tucked up snug and warm the snails have a very magical trick. They can zip and zap as fast as the fastest beetle! But they never let on to the human folk of their super zip-zap speed! That is why in the morning sunlight you see all those shiny snail trails, criss-crossing everywhere. More than likely this is only one snail, zip-zapping around your garden, munching and crunching their way through your tasty lettuce, cabbage and all manor tasty garden treats the human folk plant for them. This also amuses the Garden Fae so much, back and forth, back and forth. A very funny game so the Garden Fae think! The snails do not find it in anyway funny. And grumble at the Garden Fae. The Garden Fae often sneak up to the window and wave at Fairy, but they do not really need to. You see old ones; grown-ups don't see the Fairy Folk anymore. They are too busy with themselves, work more to get more, buying more, eating more and so on and so on. They do not see magic anymore. But sometimes little ones do, they see the Fairy Folk and all the magic that goes on right under grown-up's large noses.

This how Fairy lives her magical life, safe and warm and all the Garden Fae, birds, foxes, squirrels, hedgehogs and all manner of creatures as friends.

Sometimes she longs to be a real Garden Fae. To be able to jump off her toadstool and run and play in the garden too. It is not so bad to have dreams, to have hopes and if you work hard and with just a little bit of magic those dreams and hopes do sometimes come true.

There also is then the sad time, the Fairy sees Fred and June become old. She knows that human folk do this. They are born, tiny little creatures, squeaking and squawking, they grow and become pesky little mess makers, then the grow even more into grumpy, grumbling teenagers and then grumpy, grumbling oldies. But they also grow old-old and then they have to leave. Fairy does not know where they go when they leave, but she knows how sad everyone is when they go. And so, Fred and June leave, human folk call it dying, or passing away and their family have only memories of them then. Just like the artist, Fred and June leave Fairy alone. Their home becomes still and quiet and she knows that soon she will be taken from her lovely home. The Garden Fae are sad, the snails not so much. They don't have to make the zip-zapping sneaking journey back to the garden anymore.

This human folk time is very sad but it is how the magic works. Life is a gift of magic, each life gifted by magics and no one has a given right to this magic, so remember to think of this each day. Each morning when you open your eyes, it may be sunny and warm or cold and snowy, but each new day think – each day is a gift of the magics of our world and it is not a given right. Treasure the good days and happy days, work through the bad days and sad days, but always, always remember the gift you have been given.

One bright winters day the children of Fred and June come and start to pack things away. Each of them takes home things they love, a picture, an ornament and other things that remind them of their parents. Fairy thinks this is good, the children will see those things and remember Fred and June. Many things are taken in a big van, they go to a place where children are very poorly and they sell these things and the money is used to give these children things they wish to do. They might want to see Mickey Mouse in Disneyland or swim with dolphins in the warm sea. You see these children will not grow old so the place called Bluebell Wood makes sure they have good fun times. Fairy knows Fred and June would have liked this; other people get some of their nice things but most of all children get to have good fun times.

One day a young man called John comes in. Fairy has seen him lots of times, even when he was a cheeky young chap. But now he is a daddy too and he has such a special little girl called Adeline. He loves his lovely daughter so much and her mummy too, Heidi. They all live in a big house in the countryside, not too far from Fred and June's house. Adeline also lives with her grand-parents, Heidi's mum and dad and four dogs, yes four dogs! They all share this big house in the countryside. This means baby Adeline always has a home which is filled with love and happiness. And four doggy-smelling doggies!

The reason John has come is also to collect some of his nan and grandad's nice things so he too can have some things to look at each day and remember Nan June and Grandad Fred. He chooses some things then he sees tiny Fairy on the fire mantle and thinks, 'I think my little Adeline would like that on her window sill and when she is grown-up, we can tell her about her Great Grandma and Grandad.' He smiles at the tiny white and bronze Fairy. He thinks she is very pretty and so delicate. 'We will have to take good care of you, won't we now?' He carefully wraps her up in the poppy-bubble-popping wrap and puts her in the box with the other things.

Fairy is suddenly out of the poppy-bubble-popping wrap and sees a young woman looking at her.

'Oh, she is pretty and so well made.' Heidi says and knows the perfect place for her. She sits
Fairy on the bright window sill that looks out over their big country garden, Fairy can see the fields and woods beyond. She thinks this is a good place, she will see the Garden Fae and all the Woodland Fae too. She will see them making the dew drops that they drop onto the spidery-webs and on the green grass. She will see them telling the spring daffodils, who I must point out, are very lazy and do not like to leave their warm earth beds, to wake up and show their yellow faces. For it is spring and time they were up and about. But as I said they are so very lazy and she knows the Garden Fae will have to really shout at them. Not so the snowdrop, they are soon up and about, even if the Fae have not cleared all the snow away, they are often up. Fairy also will see all the woodland folk too. The darting, running, scampering squirrels, the plodding, snuffling hedgehogs and all the other woodland folk. Yes, Fairy thought this is a nice home and did not feel too sad now at leaving the home of June and Fred. Like

16

the human-folk she would always remember them and the artist too. It was nice to be loved and have a lovely home again too.

'That looks great there.' Said John as he came into the nursery, baby Adeline wrapped in her big strong daddy builder's arms. A room which was filled with all nice things a baby loves; toys and pretty clothes and most of all her mummy and daddy!

'Yeah, plus little fingers won't be able to reach it for some time.' Heidi said

But little baby Adeline had seen Fairy, but not the shiny white and bronzed-winged fairy we would see. Baby Adeline gurgled at the tiny fairy as Fairy turned and smiled at her. Fairy thought she might fall off her toadstool. Baby Adeline saw her, and I mean to say, Baby Adeline sees the magic Fairy that the Queen of The Fae had granted her. To Baby Adeline, Fairy was as real as her four doggies that ran riot in their home. Though far more pretty, less hairy and less stinky! Fairy could now leap of her toadstool, run in the garden and as Adeline grew and began human folk talk, Fairy could chat away the days with her. And fairy could chat, chatter, gossip, prattle-prattle all day long. Even to the point where Adeline would point to her sticky tape. Fairy would know Adeline was threatening to sticky-up her Fairy mouth for some peace and quiet. Fairy always knew that Adeline would not really sticky-up her mouth, but it was a funny kind of way to get the message across. Too much chat, chatter, gossip and prattle-prattle!

The years tick by, tick-tock, day by day, week by week, month by month and year by year. And soon that gurgling, messy pretty babe called Adeline grows. Soon crawling and walking and then talking. Oh, so many questions, mummy Heidi and daddy John think their brains might melt. But this is what young ones do, and they have to know, must know, everything in the world, but baby Adeline would always be different and it would take many years before she understood this. Adeline was soon a grown-up 6-year old sat at her desk which looked out towards the window and the big country garden and the woodlands beyond. She was so busy one bright summers day. It was Sunday, so her mum and dad (no mummy and daddy, she was grown-up now!), nan and grandad, even Rosie, Bella, Freddie (wonder where that name came from, Freddie being a rather, extra porky dog!), and Molly were all still snoring, grunting and dreaming in their Sunday beds. Everyone deserves a long snooze on Sunday, in fact I am sure it is the Law! But Adeline was not, she was wrapped in her pretty pink night gown warm and snuggy-wuggy, sat at her desk. Her drawing book open, her crayons and pencils strewn all over. She was busy drawing and colouring the bright daffodils, (yes, they had finally been shouted out of their earthy beds by the Woodland Fae.). Adeline loved to draw, colour and paint and she was very good at it.

Two teeny-tiny feet suddenly appeared, just where she was carefully colouring the brightest yellow of her daffodil petals.

'Good morning!' Adeline said most politely, as Fairy has always taught her to be most polite just as Mr Jerimiah Jeffrey Johnson Jones had been.

'It is such a pretty morning. Shall we go in the garden?'

'Oh, that would be….' But Adeline remembered her mum and dad and their stern faces as they told her she must not go downstairs on her own, she must be sure that one or more grown-up should be up too, 'I can't.' she groaned.

'I cannot, tch!' said Fairy.

'Mum and dad will be angry if I go out when no one is up.'

'Well, they only want you to be safe,' Fairy said and climbed on her toadstool and gazed out longingly at the lovely morning. Before Adeline had woken, just as Mr Sun had peeped over the hill, she had waved at the Garden Fae. They were dancing through the grass, their baskets full of diamond dew drops and they were throwing them out of their baskets onto the spidery webs and grass. As Mr Sun rose the dew twinkled like the finest diamonds. But Fairy knew that a diamond was nothing to the sparkle of a misty summer mornings dew. The dew sparkled and tickled the grass and leaves as it ran down the springy green leaves. It was like they were having a soft shower and then into the soft earth the dew trickled, a lovely cold drink for all the garden before Mr Sun grew warm. The sheep and cows and all other grass-munching creatures also welcomed the tasty green grass covered with fresh, clean water. Very tasty! Like a fat croissant and fresh orange that human folk loved to gobble for breakfast, very tasty!

And this is how Fairy and Adeline spoke each morning, sometimes, well most times Adeline had no time at all as she had to go to school to learn all the things that human-folk thought they should know. Reading words, adding numbers and all manner of things that Fairy, well if truth be told, was not really interested in. She loved just to sit and watch the changing seasons. How all the Fairy-Folk would work to see each season was never late, or in the case of daffodils, never lazy.

     I think Fairy had a dream of being one of those Fairy-Folk. Tending and caring for all manner of nature's plants and creatures. So sometimes I think our Fairy may have been a little sad. I think our Fairy wished that the Queen of the Fae would use her magic and make her a real Woodland Fae. And as you know when we dream of things like this, we can become sad too as our hearts wish for these dreams and fancies to become real and true. And in most of these cases our dreams, wishes and hopes do not come true. But we also have to find happiness in what we have and not in the longings of what we would have! But we should always dream and hope but at the same time, always remember these for what they are, they are things we hope for and not to be too sad when they do not happen. That we may have so much to be happy for even if a dream fades away.

Night time was good too, when Adeline would be squeaky clean from all the scrubbing in the big bathy-tub that mum would fill with lovely smelly bubbles. Mum would tuck her up, snuggly warm under her unicorn bed cover and then give her a big kiss. Dad would come then, yawning away as he was tired from building the big houses that everyone needed. He would snuggle up and read her lovely tales. Fairy would sneak under the covers and tickle Adeline's toes and make her wriggle. Her dad would tickle her too and call her 'wriggly-bum'. Which was a naughty word but it was their secret!

'Right, kiddo. What story tonight….'

'Freddie and the Fairy please….'

'As if I didn't know!'

'Daaaaaad'

'OK, OK!' and he would tickle her ribs. He had laughed at the book Heidi had bought. She said she couldn't help it. It was the title! And as we know Adeline's Great-Grandad was called Fred and often called our Freddie by his family. So, Adeline kind of thought that Freddie in the book was her Great-Grandad when he was not a Mega-Mega-Ancient.

'I like to think it is Great-Grandad as a boy who can't speak well and how it messes up his wishes with the poor Fairy who cannot hear well. My Fairy always tells me to speak properly and always listen and listen and listen.'

'Well your Fairy must be a very good fairy as speaking properly means that you will be heard too! And listening means you also....'

'are paying attention to what other people need to say, and hearing their feelings?'

'Yeah, kiddo. You are a real smarty-pants.' And tickled her again.

Fairy loved these moments, mum, dad and Adeline moments. Adeline would always be one of those Human Folk that other, Human Folk would want to be with. She would always listen to them and then would usually, and in most cases, especially those where people were sad, she would know just the right words to make them feel better or words that would help them to solve all those Human Kind problems. All because she took the time to listen.

Like yesterday in school her best friend had asked 'Should I kiss Danny?' (yucky-yuck-yuck, a girl of her sophistication ((Adeline had heard that word from mum)) kissing a grubby, smelly boy, yucky-yuck-yuck). Her best friend had most whole-heartily agreed, yuck! And most importantly, what party dress to wear at her7[th] birthday party? Now that was a serious question, Adeline had thought the lovely blue velvet as it looked so sophisticated! And of course, her best friend had whole-heartily agreed. I think that maybe Adeline and her best friend Isabella might not quite know what 'Sophisticated' means but it worked for them!

So, most nights ended up with Freddie and the Fairy and lots and lots of giggles before Adeline would fall fast asleep. Safe, warm and happy. But just sometimes Adeline and the Fairy did have some adventures and Fairy had some of own as well!

The Mean Moggie!

There are many creatures in this world but nothing like the cat. A fierce, scratchy, meowy creature that at one moment is so cute, so cuddly, purring in your arms. Then it is a creature of disdain and contempt. The cat is truly as fickle as Human Folk and if you have had the pleasure of a cat allowing you to give it a home and all the creature comforts that you should provide for it then you know exactly what I mean. And then there is Mean-Moggie, and this name was given for very, very good reason. Mean-Moggie is black, all over apart from one tiny white spot on one of his ears. He is proud and saunters around his kingdom. His kingdom being the neighbour's home of Adeline. Mrs Partridge loves her cat, she named him Arthur and, in my opinion, a far too noble a name for this proudful creature. But Mr Partridge who sees this cat for what he is, proud, mean and scratchy, meowy and bitey, well he named him Mean-Moggie.

But of course, he never said this name in front of Mrs Partridge, for he knew how much she loved her cat and never, ever saw his faults. But maybe she preferred to ignore them. This is sometimes what grown-ups do. They see only what they want to see and that is one reason why grown-ups do not see fairies or magic. So, this strutting, scratchy, bitey and proud cat was never shown that his mean ways were not how you should behave.

But Fairy saw them. And Fairy set about teaching this proudful, mean cat a lesson on being kind and fair.

You see one day Adeline was busy at her desk drawing and colouring and Fairy sat on the edge of her paper, all crossed legged and gibber-jabbering on. When there was such a commotion!

'Whoof, yelp and whoof.' Molly the oldest and laziest of the dogs of Adeline's residence was whoofing and yelping around and around the great beach tree in the garden. You see on fine warm days Molly loved nothing more than plodding into the garden and snoozing under the beach tree. But at this very moment was now whoofing and yelping and running around and around the tree.

'Well that is strange, what has upset Molly so?' Adeline said staring down at Molly and her commotion.

'It was Mean-Moggie!' Glowered Fairy, very angry at what she had just seen!

'Mean-Moggie, what has the horrid cat done to poor old Molly?' Even Adeline and Fairy knew the name Mr Partridge had given the cat and quite rightly so in their opinion.

'There was Molly, snoozing and snoring and whoofing in her sleep (as dogs do) and that mean cat sneaked up and bit the very end of poor Molly's fluffy, waggy tail!' said Fairy who was now very cross, 'What a mean and horrid thing to do. And then he ran up the tree, snickering at poor Molly who of course had been so rudely awakened and her poor fluffy, waggy tail was stinging.'

'I think it is time to teach Mean-Moggie some lessons.'

'Oh, I so think so too, because this is not the first time this horrid creature has done nasty tricks. Stealing the farm kittens' food. You know he even did a whopsie in the bird bath. Then climbing in windows and knocking things off shelves so they smash in hundreds of pieces. Scratching at sofas and doors. Poor hedgehog was rolled around the garden like a football!'

'He is truly not a nice creature, but how do we teach him that being nasty is so wrong and especially when old Mrs Partridge will have nothing said against her precious Arthur (Mean-Moggie to us)?'

'Sometimes to be on the receiving end of a nasty trick is about the only way to go about dealing with a creature like this, full of pride and spoilt and never shown what is the right way to behave. I will have to have serious mind-matter use on this one!' And Fairy settled on her toadstool to use all her mind-matter to give Mean-Moggie a good lesson.

Meanwhile, Mean-Moggie carried on snickering at poor Molly totally unaware that others were plotting a nasty trick on this proudful and mean cat.

A few days later and lots of mind-matter use.

'Have you got it?' Fairy jumped excitedly and jibber-jabbered her list of items she needed to Adeline.

'Yes, I will get them for you, but what on earth do you want Extra-Volcano-Super-Hot Chilli paste for, I cannot imagine.' Adeline said as she left her desk to get the jar of Extra-Volcano-Super-Hot Chilli paste and soon returned placing it on the desk.'

'You will see, but I have to talk to Molly.' Fairy said grinning at the bright red jar filled with the Extra-Volcano-Super-Hot Chilli paste.

And Fairy scampered off to find Molly who had now taken to snoozing, snoring and whoofing in her sleep in her soft comfy bed in the warm kitchen. Missing going out under the great beach tree, but remembering all too well that nasty bite and how sore it had been. It was Adeline who had gently bathed her sore fluffy, waggy tail and put some white gooey stuff on that took away the sting.

'Hello Molly!' Fairy whispered in the dog's ear. Dogs can see and hear fairies. So next time you see a dog chasing his tail, round and round, look again you just might see a fairy zipping round and round too as dogs and fairies love to play round and round chasey! Such good fun!

'Hello there, not up to round and round chasey today.' Molly said in doggy talk of course!

'Oh, I have not come to play today. How would you like to give Mean-Moggie a taste of his own nasty tricks?'

'Oh, that would be so fine.'

'Well here's the plan....'

And so, the plan was planned, the plot stirred and mixed and Mean-Moggie would soon be receiving some of what he liked to dish out.

The next bright and sunny day the planned plan was set into plan!

'Mmm, where is Molly today?' thought Mean-Moggie and then sniggered. 'Perhaps she is taking her afternoon nap indoors now.' Which kind of disappointed him, he would have to find some other creature to torment. How he loved to push around the tiny farm kittens and gobble all their food. Or maybe paying a visit to the old and batty Mrs Bird down the road and knocking and smashing one of those horrid dog figurines she loved would be a good afternoons fun. But; he climbed up the great beach tree and thought maybe a snooze was in order. Mean-Moggie was also very lazy. And on a nice afternoon as this why bother to do anything. Mrs Partridge would have his favourite dinner ready soon, fresh warm tasty chicken and tasty rich fresh cream to wash it all down. And he began to purr softly as he snoozed the afternoon away.

'Come on Molly, he's up in the tree.' Fairy whispered to Molly. Adeline up in her room, busy, busy doing her homework noticed the creeping, sneaking Fairy and Molly slowly creeping and sneaking until they were under the great beach tree. It was then she noticed Mean-Moggie snoozing on a very comfy branch above them.

'What are those two up to?' and began to watch the goings on intently.

'Right you lie down and I will fix it on.'

'OK.' And Molly quietly settled down on the soft green grass. She stretched out her fluffy waggy tail and Fairy set about the sneaky punishment for Mean-Moggie. The Fairy hid herself away in the long grass to wait. Her little heart was pounding and for a moment and only a moment thought that what they had planned might be seen as very naughty by the other fairies.

Mean-Moggie snoozed and then opened one of his green eyes. 'Ah, there you are Molly dog, it seems you have found your courage to come out again!'

Slinking, creeping, slithering went Mean-Moggie down the tree trunk. Careful paws, carefully sneaked nearer and nearer. Tippy-toe, silent and sneaking crept the cat. His cat face smirking at the stupid dog.

THEN!

MEOWING, SCREECHING, PANTING, RACING

LAUGHING, WHOOFING, GIGGLING, BIG-WHOOFY-WHOOFS

Adeline looked upon all the noise.
Cat was running.
Molly was chasing.
Fairy was giggling and rolling in the grass.
Oh, poor Mean-Moggie!

You see it is usually those that are mean, who play nasty tricks that yell and cause the most horrendous commotions when they have finally have had their comeuppance and Mean-Moggie had got his today.

Oh, he went sneaking and creeping up to Molly. Opened his jaws and sank his pearly white fangs into poor Molly's fluffy waggy tail.

Suddenly, STICKY, HOT, HOTTER, AND EVEN HOTTER. THEN EVEN-MORE-HOTTER, EXTRA-VOLCANO-SUPER-HOT-CHILLI-PASTE HOT!!!!!!!

That little Fairy had made a plan and that plan had worked. Finding one of Adeline's party balloons and oh-so carefully squeezing the paste into the small white shiny balloon. Carefully tying it to Molly's fluffy waggy tail, pulling and tidying her soft white fur over it.

Now Mean-Moggie had a mouth full of the Extra-Volcano-Super-Hot Chilli paste. His mouth hot, and it was as if you could see steam popping out of his ears. Farm kittens were cat-howling as Mean-Moggie ran around and around the great beach tree. Molly sat watching, thinking how do you like a taste of your own medicine and whoofy-giggled at her own joke. All the other creatures, birds that he had chased and whoopsied in their bird bath, hedgehogs he had rolled and rolled around the garden, squirrels he had chased and dug up their winter stores of acorns, all those creatures came and watched as Mean-Moggie found out what it was to have a nasty trick played on him!

'They are so mean and horrid.' Thought Mean-Moggie, well mean and horrid it was but now cat knew what mean and horrid meant and now as he saw all the creatures laughing at his hot-hotter mouth, he knew what he must do. He would have to mend his ways and perhaps the creatures would forgive him and they could all get along just fine. But Mean-Moggie was so very proudful that he ran and ran as far as he could until he was lost and far away from his home. He was far too proud, too spoilt to every say sorry, to ever ask to be forgiven and that he would mend his ways!

Adeline watched all this and thought that well maybe the horrid cat deserved his punishment but maybe, just maybe it may make Mean-Moggie far worse. But she had to giggle though, he did look rather funny racing round the garden trying to cool his mouth.

Sometimes these plans work, they make those of mean spirits think about how it feels to receive some nasty treatment or what it is like to have nasty cruel things said about them that hurt people on the inside. But as the fairies would tell you if you could still see them this is not always the case. Some will be so hurt they will become more-cruel and mean. Others will be so hurt that they will run away, just like Mean-Moggie. They will tell you to be so very careful and sometimes you need to see, really see why some creatures are nasty and listen, really listen as they may have never been shown how mean they are and that is it wrong.

And that day Mean-Moggie ran away!

What became of Mean Moggie is another tale!

The End for now!

Printed by Amazon Italia Logistica S.r.l.
Torrazza Piemonte (TO), Italy